To Master Vo, whose training and guidance
help ninjas go where they want to go!
XOXO Ka

Where Do Ninjas Go On Vacation?

Published by Lucky Four Press, LLC, 2022
Copyright ©2022 Kim Ann / Lucky Four Press, LLC
Library of Congress Number: 2022908787

Inquiries should be directed to: luckyfourpress@yahoo.com
or to the author at: kim@kimann.co.

www.kimann.co

ISBN-13: 978-1-953774-35-4 Paperback
ISBN-13: 978-1-953774-37-8 Hardback

Where Do Ninjas Go on Vacation?

by Kim Ann

Illustrated by

Nejla Shojaie

Where do ninjas go
when they just want to disappear?

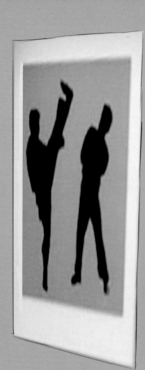

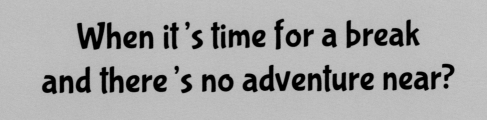

When it's time for a break
and there's no adventure near?

Do ninjas like the desert and cruising through the sand?

Driving monster trucks up mountains
and across the land?

Do ninjas like to ride rides
at bright and happy places?

And play basketball undercover
in open spaces?

Do ninjas dream of giant castles up in the clouds?

Swimming pools with diving boards.
They're hiding from the crowds!

Do ninjas like pretty things
like flowers, trees, and plants?

Can they be found in their gardens
when they have a chance?

Do ninjas like playing games
and laughing out loud too?

They like telling jokes the way
that only they can do?

When ninjas go on vacation,
are they together?

Or do they go their own way,
then gather whenever?

If we spot a ninja—
which is difficult; that's true—

we can ask about the others
and maybe get a clue.

Kim Ann

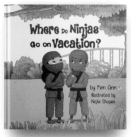

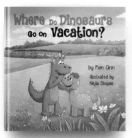

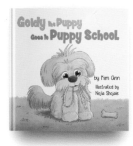

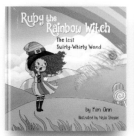

ruby,
la brujita arcoiris

Coloring
Books

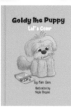